Lots of surprises are
for Dilo when he ret
Lighthouse Ba

Pat who lives in the
lighthouse has a tame
seagull, Silver, who has
only one leg.

A visit by the Terrible Twins,
Debra and Robin, should be
trouble free. But it isn't.

Dilo finds himself in
mortal danger when
disaster strikes a rig
exploring for oil.

Horace Dobbs

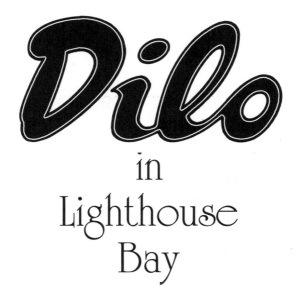

in
Lighthouse
Bay

illustrated by
Rico

Watch

Publishing

Watch Publishing
'Dolphin'
10 Melton Road
North Ferriby
East Yorkshire
HU14 3ET
Tel: 01482 632650
Fax: 01482 634914
Email: horace@drdobbs.karoo.co.uk
Website: www.idw.org

ISBN
0 9541721 4 0
© Horace Dobbs 2006

Printed by
Redcliff Print & Design
30 The Weir
Hessle
East Yorkshire
HU13 0RU
Tel: 01482 640428
Fax: 01482 641390

Contents
Dilo in Lighthouse Bay

THE END

To Jackie and Terry Connell
for all they have done to
help children with special needs.

1 The Penguin

Debra and Robin were known as the Terrible Twins for good reason. They had a habit of getting into mischief. They didn't mean it. It just seemed to happen.

There was the day their mother took them to the zoo in her ancient car. It was the beginning of the summer holidays. The two children loved seeing the animals. But they didn't like to think of them being held in captivity. At the end of the afternoon, Mary, that was their mother's name, took Debra and Robin to the penguin house. It was a messy, smelly place with a shallow pool.

"It will soon be time to go home. Will you stay here while I go and get myself a cup of tea?"

"Yes Mum," the twins replied in unison.

"And don't get into any mischief."

As they watched her disappear the twins had every intention of being good. But somehow it didn't work out.

When she returned Mary was horrified when she saw the state of her children. They were filthy.

"What on earth have you been doing?" she asked, not expecting a reply. "You're both covered in dirt. I'll have to take you home straight away and get you into a bath."

For once the twins didn't argue with her. They brushed themselves down and scrambled into the car.

"You two are unusually quiet," said Mary as the car rattled homewards.

Robin held both hands against a lump under his mud spattered sweatshirt. Debra looked at him. The lump moved a bit and then stayed still.

"We've had a lovely time Mum, really we have," responded Debra, finding it hard not to giggle.

When they arrived home Robin, who normally didn't like washing, made his way straight to the bathroom. His mother was delighted with this unexpected turn of good behaviour.

"I'll bring you some clean clothes," she shouted up the stairs.

"Don't bother Mum, I'll take them up," offered Debra.

"Oh thank you Debbie," replied Mary, beginning to get slightly suspicious. Then she noticed Debra trying to suppress a smirk.

"Are you sure you two are not up to something?" she asked.

At that point the sound of splashing came from the bathroom. Mary gathered up some clothes for Robin and gave them to her daughter. Without thinking she followed Debra upstairs to the bathroom and knocked on the door.

"Come in," came a voice from inside.

Robin's mother opened the bathroom door

and stared in amazement. She couldn't believe her eyes. Robin was still in his dirty clothes.

"What's that?" she screamed, pointing at a small penguin paddling around in murky water at the bottom of the bath.

At exactly that moment the startled creature decided to try to escape. It jumped up and managed to clamber over the side of the bath. In a flurry of muddy water the penguin landed in a heap on the floor. It then righted itself, flapped it's stumpy wings and had a good shake, showering dirty water over Mary and the bathroom. The penguin then stood quite still, looked up and stared dolefully at Robin's mother.

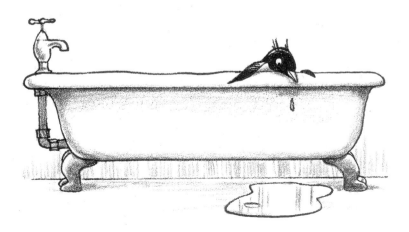

"We felt sorry for it all locked up in that smelly zoo," said Robin. "We thought Percy would be much happier back in the sea where he belongs. We want to take him to Uncle Pat's. He rescues birds."

"Percy, Percy," shrieked his mother who was still in a state of shock. "What do you mean Percy?"

"Percy the penguin," replied Robin with the special look he used when he knew he had done something wrong but wanted to appear innocent.

"How stupid can you get?" yelled Robin's mother. " How on earth can I let you go to Uncle Pat's next week if you are going to behave like this? I've a good mind to cancel your visit to Lighthouse Bay."

"Oh Mum, you can't do that," cried Debra with horror.

"Oh yes I can," said Mary wagging a finger at her children.

Debra realised her mother was very angry.

Drastic action was needed. She spread her mouth and rubbed her eye. A tear trickled down her cheek.

"It was Robin's idea," she said, sobbing.

"You can stop acting my girl. You were both in it together. I know you were."

"We want to take Percy with us to Uncle Pat's, He's an expert on birds and wildlife. He'll help us put Percy back in the wild where he belongs," pleaded Robin.

"Oh no he won't. Percy, I mean that penguin, is going back to the zoo."

"But Mum!" they cried together.

"But Mum nothing," came the sharp retort.

By the time a van arrived to remove the penguin Mary had calmed down. She could see the funny side of the situation. But the curator of the zoo was not amused. He threatened to report the children to the police if Mary did not pay his expenses for coming to collect the penguin.

2   Dilo Cake

The twins knew that there was not much money to spare since their father had left their mother to bring up the children on her own. Debra and Robin decided they would have to do something really special to make-up. They secretly emptied the box of money they had been saving up for their holiday in Lighthouse Bay.

After their mother left for work the next day the twins went to the shops. They bought a sponge, some candles and a squeezy bottle of chocolate sauce.

"It's very messy," said Debra when they got back home and she was dribbling runny chocolate onto a slice of bread to practice.

When Debra had finished Robin said, "That's good. I'll eat this piece while you do the cake."

Debra gave Robin one of her special looks as she moved towards the sponge. Quickly a dolphin shape appeared. Then she added some wiggles for waves.

"We can use a currant for an eye," said Robin, licking his fingers.

"Now for the tricky bit," said Debra nervously biting her lip. "Dee, Eye, Elle, Oh."

"It's a bit wobbly, but it will do," commented Robin.

Shortly after the Dilo cake was finished the twins heard a key turn in the front door.

"Quick, quick, I'll light the candle," said Robin.

As soon as it was lit Debra rushed to greet her mother.

"My, my you look excited," Mary exclaimed as she walked into the hall, dropping a bag of heavy shopping onto the floor.

"Shut your eyes and come with me," said

Debra taking her mother's hand and leading her along the hall.

"You can open them now," said Robin when they reached the kitchen.

When Mary opened her eyes they were wide with amazement.

"Oh twins," she said with unsuppressed joy. "It's absolutely beautiful. What a lovely cake. Shall I blow out the candle?"

"Yes!" the twins cried in unison. "And make a wish at the same time," added Debra.

"What's this?" said their mother, picking up a handwritten note from beside the cake. She read it aloud. "Dear Mum we are sorry about the penguin. With lots of love from Debra and Robin. Kiss. Kiss. Kiss." Mary rubbed a tear from the corner of her eye.

Mary looked at the cake and then at Debra. She knew how much Dilo the dolphin meant to her daughter.

"I know you had some wonderful times with

Dilo in Lighthouse Bay and you desperately want to see the dolphin again. But in his last letter Uncle Pat said there have been no sightings of Dilo since he was captured and then set free from the aquarium at Crookhaven. We all hoped Dilo would make his way back to the bay. But it doesn't look like he's going to."

Mary could see this upset her daughter. So she said something that she hoped would cheer Debra up. "Uncle Pat says he's got a seagull that has become very tame. Apparently it sits on the lighthouse wall and lets Pat feed it by hand. He calls it Silver."

"That's a funny name for a seagull," said Robin.

"That's because it's only got one leg," explained his mother. "He named it after Long John Silver in the book Treasure Island."

"But Long John Silver had a parrot, not a seagull."

"Don't be silly Robin you know what Mum

means. Long John Silver only had one leg."

"No he didn't. He had two. Only one of them was made of wood."

"That's enough of that you two! It's early to bed for you tonight. You've got to get up early tomorrow if you are going to catch the train to Lighthouse Bay."

Debra was so excited she couldn't sleep. As she lay in her bed Debra thought about Lighthouse Bay. In her mind she saw her Uncle Pat leaning on the wall outside the lighthouse gazing out to sea. Beside him was his cat, Sprat, and his dog, Boka, who followed him everywhere. Now Pat had a new companion, Silver, the one legged seagull.

Just before she dropped off to sleep Debra gazed at the moon out of her bedroom window. As she watched, a falling star flashed across the heavens. To Debra it was a signal from Dilo.

Debra had heard someone say that when you see a falling star you should make a wish. So she made a wish. The hardest wish she possibly could.

And she sent it to Dilo. "Please, please Dilo, please come back to Lighthouse Bay."

3 Dilo

Dilo the dolphin had a problem. He was nosy. Even when he was very young Dilo always wanted to know what was going on. The first time he poked his nose, or more correctly his beak, into a small cave to find out what was inside, he got a nasty shock. The cave was the home of a lobster who didn't like visitors. And the lobster nipped his nose.

Dilo also loved to roam. "The Call of the Deep", was what his mother called it. At first Dilo didn't realise what this meant. But as he grew older he did. He would always be on the move - like a gypsy or a nomad.

As soon as Dilo was old enough he and his mother set off on a long journey. They had many adventures along the way before she was accidentally killed in a net.

Dilo was feeling lonely on the night that Debra was looking at the moon out of her bedroom window. Far away Dilo was looking at the same moon and saw the same falling star. He didn't know why, but for some reason Dilo started to think about Debra and the fun they had swimming and playing together. But not all of his memories of Lighthouse Bay were happy ones. He also remembered being lured into a net near Black Rock and taken to an aquarium. For Dilo it was like being in prison. Locked up in the pool Dilo could still feel the Call of the Deep. He longed to be back in the open sea. Dilo jumped for joy when Debra and her friends came to his rescue and set him free.

Back again in the open sea Dilo enjoyed going on journeys more than ever. He loved exploring new places. But something inside Dilo was pulling him back to Lighthouse Bay.

"Shall I go, or shan't I go?" he asked

himself.

Suddenly he made a decision. With a powerful thrust of his tail Dilo sped forward. He was on his way back to Lighthouse Bay.

4 Uncle Pat

As soon as the train stopped in Lighthouse Bay, Debra opened the door and leapt out. She looked down the platform. In the distance was her Uncle Pat. Debra jumped up and down waving her arms. Pat saw her and waved back. Debra ran towards him.

"Hey Debra," yelled a voice from behind her. It was Robin. "What about your bags?"

Debra turned her head but continued running.

"Put them on the platform. I'll come back for them."

Debra rushed up to her uncle who was walking towards her. She threw her arms around him and gave him a hug.

"Oh, it's lovely to see you again Uncle Pat."

Debra took her uncle's hand and the two walked along the platform to where Robin was standing by the baggage. Actually Pat walked, Debra danced alongside him, waving her arms with excitement.

"Is there any news of Dilo?" asked Robin as they set off.

"Everyone is keeping a look out but there have been no sightings."

"That's because he's been waiting for us to come back," said Debra optimistically.

She was convinced that the dolphin would return. Robin did not share his twin's optimism.

Secretly Pat thought the chances of Dilo returning were very slight. But he didn't want to dampen Debra's hopes. So he changed the subject. He was leading the way to the harbour.

"We're going to Mike's boat. She's moored alongside the harbour wall. Mike said he would run us out to the lighthouse steps in his inflatable."

Debra's eyes lit up. Mike was one of Debra's very special grown-up friends. He was a professional diver. He always said Debra was a natural swimmer. "A proper little mermaid" was how he described her. He had even taught Debra to use an aqualung. She was looking forward to sharing more adventures under the sea with him.

Robin, on the other hand, couldn't swim. He did not want to learn. He was scared of the sea but would not admit it to his sister.

Robin's great passion in life was computers. In fact you could say Robin was very good with computers. Not just at computer games, but using them to solve problems and to store data.

Robin was able to put his computer skills to good use when his uncle became a warden for International Wildlife Watch. One of Pat's jobs was to record wildlife in the area. Robin had helped his uncle to set-up a computer programme to do this. The records they compiled turned out to be very valuable because lots of changes were taking place in the bay - as Robin and Debra were shortly to find out.

5 Merlin

"Ahoy Mike," called Debra when they reached Mike's diving boat Merlin, which was tied up alongside the quay.

"Come aboard," shouted Mike who was coiling a rope on the deck. "I've been expecting you."

They all gathered in the wheelhouse, Debra was very pleased to be back on board Merlin. So too was Robin. He looked around with glee at all the dials and recorders.

"I've got a new instrument that may interest you," said Mike.

Robin's eyes lit up.

"What is it?" he asked.

"It's called a hydrophone. It's an underwater microphone. The Navy use them for detecting

enemy submarines. If there are any dolphins around I can hear them."

"Oh please turn it on," said Debra, "perhaps we can hear Dilo!"

Mike switched on the hydrophone. He turned up the volume. Lots of different sounds came out of a loudspeaker.

"It shows the sounds here," said Mike, pointing to a jagged line flickering on a screen.

"Dolphins make sounds we can't hear," said Robin.

"I know that!" said Debra, "They're called ultrasounds. Dilo can use them to see inside things."

Robin was most impressed with his twin sister's knowledge.

"I thought you weren't interested in gadgets," he commented,

"I am if they can help us find Dilo," Debra replied indignantly.

"This machine is very clever," continued

Mike. "It can turn sounds we can't hear into sounds we can."

"Like dolphin's sonar?" asked Robin

"Yes," replied Mike.

The twins watched and listened intently. Mike turned various knobs and clicked switches. The sounds changed and the screens flickered.

"I'm sorry to disappoint you Debra, there are no sonar signals" said Mike. "Dilo's not here."

"He may not be here yet, But he's going to come. I know he is," said Debra bravely.

Mike continued to operate the hydrophone. The screen flickered wildly. The sounds from the loudspeaker changed abruptly. 'Grr Grr,' a deep grinding noise filled the wheelhouse.

"That may be why Dilo's not here," said Mike.

"What is it?" asked Robin and Debra in unison.

Before Mike could answer the sound was cut off. An urgent message was coming through.

The 'Grr Grr' sound was forgotten.

"Platform Delta calling Merlin Diver. Over," came the sharp sound.

Mike picked up a handset.

"Merlin Diver receiving. Over."

"Can you come and pick up a crewman and take him ashore? Over."

"Yes, I'll be there in twenty minutes. Over."

"Roger Merlin Diver. Out."

A few minutes later Mike's inflatable, with Debra, Robin and their Uncle Pat onboard, was nosing out of the harbour. Once clear of the entrance Mike opened the throttle. In an instant the boat was skimming across the bay. White spray flew into the air, sparkling in the brilliant sunshine.

They soon reached the lighthouse. Mike jumped ashore and deftly tied the painter to a heavy iron ring in the rust-stained rocks. Pat held out his hand to help Robin ashore. Debra climbed onto the wall of the inflatable and jumped nimbly

onto the rocks. Mike stepped back on to the boat and handed up the baggage. Pat untied the painter and threw it onto the floor of the inflatable.

Mike had a job to do. A few moments later he was speeding away to collect a passenger from Platform Delta.

6 The Oil Rig

Dilo beamed his sonar ahead. All he could detect was sea, sea and more sea. He had made up his mind. Dilo knew exactly which way he had to go to get to Lighthouse Bay.

The sun was shining. A gentle wind raised small waves. Dilo's body glistened and the star on his dorsal fin sparkled as he bounded along. The dolphin felt as free as the wind. He was filled with joy. Dilo wondered what he would find at the end of his journey.

The sun was high in the sky when Dilo sensed he was getting near his destination. Long before he arrived he heard strange sounds. A deep vibration was coming through the water from the seabed. He knew the rumbling sounds made by rocks being moved in a wild storm. It wasn't that.

But it was just as powerful. Dilo sensed danger and wondered if he should turn around and go somewhere else. But a force inside him pulled him ever onwards towards Lighthouse Bay.

The closer he got the louder the noise became. Dilo felt excited. He turned his sonar onto full power to see what was ahead of him. His mother called his sonar his 'magic sound'. At the same time Dilo made the sound he listened for the echo. That's why sonar is sometimes called 'echo location'. On this occasion Dilo's magic sound showed him some pillars that stretched from the seabed to above the surface. They were the legs of a huge oil rig. The growling noise did not come from them. It was made by a drill that was biting its way in to the earth's crust.

Cautiously the dolphin circled the entire oil rig. He could sense no danger. He swam towards one of the giant legs. When he got close Dilo used his eyes as well as his magic sound. Slowly the image of one of the pillars emerged through the murky water. A few fishes were hanging close-by. They swam away as Dilo approached.

The dolphin hovered for a moment. Then he moved slowly towards the giant rod that was boring into the seabed. Dilo swam into a billowing cloud of silt coming up from the sea bed. It was pitch dark inside the cloud. He couldn't see with his eyes anymore. Dilo had to use his sonar. The dense underwater cloud was made up from the slurry used to lubricate the drill. It tasted strange.

Like smoke from a chimney, the water current was carrying the silt away from the drill.

Dilo headed into the current. Suddenly he was through the cloud and into clear, bright water again. Dilo could see the seabed was covered with a layer of fine white sediment. Nothing was living on it. It was like a vast desert.

"What has happened to the creatures that are buried beneath this strange barren seabed?" Dilo wondered.

The dolphin remembered how in the past he had caught flat fish in this very same area. Now there were none. Would there still be fish elsewhere?

Dilo left the giant structure behind him and headed further into Lighthouse Bay. His target was Black Rock. There were always fishes there, hiding between the jagged rocks that had taken many ships to their doom in wild storms. Local legend said that Black Rock was the home of a wicked witch who howled when strong winds blew. Today the sea was calm.

As Dilo got closer to Black Rock the noises

from the drilling rig grew fainter. Other familiar sounds came through the water. He listened to the far off 'thump, thump' of a fishing boat. The gentle sloshing of the waves against the rocks got louder as he approached Black Rock.

Dilo was just about to start hunting for fish when he heard another sound.

"Clink. Clink." There was a pause, then another, "Clink. Clink.".

Dilo knew that sound. His body filled with excitement. In an instant the dolphin forgot about the oil rig, the fishing boat and getting something to eat. Instead he raced at full speed in the direction of the clinking sound.

"Clink. Clink." There it was again.

A shoal of silver eels scattered as he flashed through them. Dilo turned his sonar onto full power. It gave him a clear sound picture of what he was speeding towards. The dolphin let out a squeak of delight. Then he sent out another message saying, "I'm coming, I'm coming!"

7 Dilo meets Debra

As soon as she had settled in at the lighthouse Debra put on her wetsuit. She hurried down the steps and swam away from the shore. She gazed down through her mask. A forest of seaweed, called kelp, stretched beneath her. Debra dived down into a gulley and picked up two stones. As she headed to the surface she banged them together with a loud crack.

Back on the surface she continued to fin away from the shore, cracking the stones together as she went. This was the way Debra had let Dilo know she was coming out to swim with him in the past. She knew he would hear it if he was nearby.

Debra stopped swimming, lifted her head above the water and looked around. The lighthouse stood proudly on the top of the cliffs.

Her uncle Pat waved to her. Small fishing boats were chugging in and out of the harbour. At the entrance to Lighthouse Bay was the dreaded Black Rock.

Beyond that was the surprise that her Uncle had told her about. Standing out of the sea on huge metal legs was an oil rig. There were buildings like small houses on it. A yellow flame flickered out of a tall chimney. A helicopter was coming in to land. It hovered for a moment before dropping down onto a landing pad. Debra watched a group of men get out one by one. They ducked under the rotor blades that were still turning. As soon as they were all clear the helicopter lifted off and sped away towards the shore.

Debra watched for a few moments. Then she stuck her face back into the sea, breathed through her snorkel tube and dived. Debra was just about to bang the stones together again when she heard a squeaking sound - like a creaking door. "Eek, eek."

Debra recognised it immediately. She had heard it many times before. It was the sound Dilo made when he was swimming towards her. A moment later her beloved dolphin zoomed into view. Debra's eyes sparkled with joy. She dropped the stones.

Dilo circled around Debra. Her hair billowed out behind her as she finned hard towards him. Dilo was as excited as Debra. He bobbed his head up and down as if to say 'Hello'. And then he raced off. It was time for a game.

Still holding her breath Debra chased after Dilo. The dolphin turned quickly and was speeding back towards her. She spun around as Dilo rushed past and stretched out her hand towards him.

Dilo turned. He sped past Debra letting her hand slide over his body as he zoomed by. Debra felt his smooth skin slip by under her fingers. Then she rushed to the surface. Debra blew out the water from her snorkel and sucked in a

lungfull of air. She was out of breath. But she wasn't going to let that stop her from going back down into Dilo's world.

Debra breathed in and out three times as hard and as quickly as she could. The next moment she dipped her head and raised her legs. Debra slid gracefully and smoothly under the sea again.

As soon as she left the surface Debra finned hard. Her ears popped. Dilo was swimming towards her head on. Debra wagged her head from side to side. Dilo did the same. Debra laughed. A stream of bubbles burst from her snorkel tube. With her arms by her sides Debra kept her legs together and swam with the dolphin stroke. Dilo moved his tail up and down at the same rate. The two friends swam side by side.

Their journey took them through a rocky gulley. Then they looped back to the surface where they both took a breath. When Debra dived again she held her arms at full length ahead of her and spun like a top. As she did so the surface and the seabed seemed to twirl around her. She remembered how Dilo used to get excited when she did this. And he did again. The next time she surfaced the dolphin rushed around her like a whirling Dervish.

The dolphin was getting more and more boisterous. So was Debra. She flung herself back underwater twisting this way and that. Sometimes she could see Dilo. Sometimes she couldn't. But Dilo could always see her. Debra surfaced breathing hard.

Dilo was exploding with energy. He couldn't keep it down. He curled underneath Debra. In the next instant the dolphin was bursting like a missile through the surface. Out of the water he flew. Then he plunged back into the sea again. Debra squealed with delight as he splashed down beside her. The instant he was beneath the surface Dilo turned. The next moment the dolphin was once again soaring over Debra's head. Five times he

jumped. Each time Debra yelled with excitement. Dilo, her Dilo, was back in Lighthouse Bay.

Debra stayed in the sea with Dilo until she could swim no more.

"Dilo, I know you could play forever," she called through her snorkel tube, "but I am absolutely exhausted. I must go back to shore."

Debra's legs felt like rubber as she swam towards the cliffs. She lifted her head to make sure she was finning in the right direction. She was. Debra saw her uncle Pat watching her from the cliff top. He had been there keeping an eye on her ever since she rushed out, leaving her brother Robin working on the computer.

When she looked up Debra could see that Pat had company. Silver, the one legged seagull, was perched on the wall beside him. Pat had rescued the gull after it's foot got tangled in a nylon fishing line. Debra waved and Pat waved back. As she did so Silver took off and zoomed down towards the sea.

"Hey, Ho Silver!" yelled Debra as the gull swooped down over her. Then with a single flip of his wings Silver soared up and away to join the squawking gulls crowding over a fishing boat.

Debra continued her swim back to shore. Dilo stayed by her side all the way to the steps at the bottom of the lighthouse path. Even when Debra climbed out he stayed close by, sorry to see her leave. Debra sat on the bottom step and rested. Far away, the cloud of gulls, joined by Silver, were swooping down to gobble the pieces of fish thrown overboard from a fishing boat that was chugging towards the jetty. Suddenly their feast was over and the gulls dispersed, squawking loudly.

Dilo continued to float just off the rocks.

"Don't worry, I'll be back again soon," said Debra as she set off to climb up the cliff.

8 Telepathy

When Debra reached the top of the cliffs Debra found that Pat had been joined by her twin brother. Pat was pointing at the oil rig. Even from a distance it looked huge. The flickering flame continued to flare from the stack.

"Did you see the helicopter?" said Pat.

"Wow, yes," said Robin excitedly before his sister could answer.

"I saw it come in to land," puffed Debra, out of breath. "And I saw Dilo!" she added triumphantly.

"I know," said Robin "We watched him jumping around you"

"I can't believe it. Dilo just turned up out of the blue. Do you think he knew you would be here?" asked Pat.

"Oh yes," said Debra utterly convinced that Dilo knew she was coming back to Lighthouse Bay.

"How do you think he knew? By telepathy?" questioned Pat with a twinkle in his eye.

"What's telepathy?" asked Robin.

"It's when two people communicate without speaking," answered Pat.

"I've never heard of telepathy," said Robin. "Can you prove it scientifically?"

"I don't think so."

"In that case I want more proof than Debbie saying that she and Dilo just communicated," said Robin emphasising the word 'communicated'.

Before Debra could argue the point Robin's mind switched to something else. He pointed to a large boat with a crane on it just outside the harbour wall.

"What's that?" he asked his uncle.

"That's a dredger. They want to expand the

harbour. Deepen the channel and let bigger ships come in. They say it's going to bring prosperity to the town."

"But that will ruin it," said Debra who loved the little harbour with it's collection of small colourful fishing boats. She wanted it to stay as it was.

"You can't stop progress," commented Robin who enjoyed teasing his sister.

Robin liked machines - especially trains. This was the next best thing. The prospect of seeing the big dredger working appealed to him.

Debra, on the other hand, loved nature. To her birds and animals were far more interesting than noisy machines.

A slight current of air rose up the cliff face. With outstretched wings a small flock of gulls were using the updraft to lift them aloft. For a moment Debra admired the way they glided effortlessly back and forth. To her it seemed they flew just for the sheer joy of it. It must be marvellous to be so free she thought.

Debra noticed how, when they were flying, the gulls twisted their heads from side to side. That made her realise that they were always on the lookout - usually for food.

As she watched, one of the gulls separated from the others. Barely moving it's wings the gull glided to the cliffs. Just like the helicopter, it hovered for a moment. Then the gull closed it's wings and dropped on to the wall and hopped on one leg towards Pat.

"Have you come to meet Robin and Debra?" asked Pat, talking to the gull. "Silver's come to say 'Hello'," he continued turning to Robin.

"How do you know that?" asked Robin

"By telepathy," replied Pat, winking secretly at Debra.

9 The Dredger

When Debra left the water Dilo still had plenty of energy left. He decided he would re-visit some of his old haunts in Lighthouse Bay. He was aware of the new monster machine in the harbour. He decided to leave investigating that until later. First he would start under the lighthouse.

It was high water. The surface was calm. There was no current. Dilo nosed among the seaweeds. The kelp plants were dark green. They were like small trees. Under the broad leaves everything was quiet and still.

Dilo was in a mischievous mood. He couldn't resist prodding things with his beak. A starfish was the first to get a nudge. It didn't respond. So Dilo moved on. He saw a sea urchin respond. So Dilo moved on. He saw a sea urchin on a kelp stalk. It was covered in spines. That was why they were sometimes called "sea hedgehogs". He couldn't resist prodding it to dislodge it. The sea urchin pricked Dilo. It didn't hurt much. It was a small price to pay for watching the sea urchin fall in slow motion down the rock face onto the sand in a gulley. Dilo followed it down wagging his head gleefully from side to side.

Dilo was now down below the level where the kelp grew. This was where the tube worms, or the "plop-plops" lived. They were like flowers in an underwater garden. Dilo knew that if the tubeworms were disturbed they would retract into their tubes with a plop - that's why he called them "plop-plops". Dilo deliberately swam very close to a carpet of tube worms. They all popped back into their homes in quick succession with lots of satisfying "plops". Dilo felt his little game was working rather well.

it would be before they came back out and he could make them plop back in again. But he didn't wait to see. He swam on to a small cave where he remembered a large lobster used to live. It was at home. He peered into the cave from a safe distance. Two feelers, or antennae, waved in front of the hole. Two eyes were watching him from inside. Two large claws were ready to give Dilo a very painful nip if he tried any of his tricks. After hovering for a few minutes the dolphin decided to look for some sport elsewhere.

At that moment there was a new noise in the harbour. It was a 'clunkety, clackety' sound. Dilo sped across the seabed to see what was happening. A big iron scoop with large metal teeth was biting into the seabed. Clouds of silt swirled up. The water around it was cloudy. Dilo turned on his sonar, or echo location, to see it more clearly. When the bucket was full of sand and silt it moved up towards the surface. As it did so a flatfish that had been resting on the sand fluttered out. Dilo zoomed

through the cloudy water and caught it. He turned it round in his mouth and swallowed the fish head first. He liked the idea of having snacks served to him in this way and snapped up several more before going up for air.

The dolphin stayed on the surface for a short time. Dilo watched as the bucket dumped its slushy load into a barge. Then it splashed back into the sea to scoop-up another load. Dilo could hear the sound of the engine and the machinery. The dolphin could also feel their vibrations as the bucket dug down into the seabed. He liked hearing and feeling new sounds. He circled round the dredger bucket that was scooping out more sand and gravel to create a new deep channel.

The dolphin swam down to where the sea bed had been scooped away. Swarms of little fish were darting around. They were feeding on the worms uncovered by the dredger.

The tide was changing. The dolphin knew this was the time when the salmon started to run.

Dilo watched the dredger pull out several more scoops. Then he set off for the headland. That was where he hoped he would find a big fish.

Dilo was not disappointed. Using his sonar he detected a salmon. The dolphin surfaced and took a quick breath. He dipped his head. Dilo thrust hard with his tail. A circle of flat water marked the place on the surface where he dived. Underwater he sped like an arrow.

The salmon sensed the danger. It changed course. The fish swam as fast as it could. But Dilo was faster. As he closed in Dilo fired a concentrated sonar beam. It stunned the fish. An instant later it was clamped in Dilo's jaws. The dolphin didn't slow. He sped onwards and upwards to the surface with his prize in his jaws. He tossed the salmon up into the air. The salmon splashed back into the sea. It thought it was free and tried to swim away. But its fate was sealed. The dolphin caught it again between his teeth. He sped back to the surface. There he flipped the fish and gulped it down head first. Fish scales hung in the water - sparkling like snowflakes. Like left-over crumbs on a table they were the only sign that Dilo had been feeding.

Dilo was pleased he had returned to Lighthouse Bay. He had swum with Debra again. There were lots of new and exciting sounds to hear and machines to look at. But as Dilo was shortly to find out - there would be a high price to pay.

10 Rescue

When darkness came Dilo cruised slowly around Lighthouse Bay. The sea was full of cracks and pops - the natural sounds of the night. The surface was flat calm. The dredger had stopped working. All the machinery was quiet but the drill was still turning on the oil rig. Far below the seabed it's teeth were biting deeper and deeper into the earth's crust. Dilo could feel the vibrations through the water. They didn't bother him. He had other things on his mind.

Dilo was watching the creatures that come out at night. A large eel appeared from a hole in the rocks It wriggled past him. Dilo was not hungry. The eel continued safely on its way. The eel was looking for food. It was in luck. A dead fish was resting on a patch of sand at the bottom of a gulley. A crab was biting at it with its claws. A host of shrimps were scurrying around the corpse picking off minute scraps with their tiny claws and stuffing them in their mouths.

Dilo hung in the water watching the scene. A lobster had also sensed the decaying fish. With its huge claws held aloft it was gliding towards the same spot to join in the feast. The eel got there first. Dilo watched as the eel grabbed the prize. The crab still clung to it's meal. The eel shook the dead fish and started to pull it towards it's lair in the rocks. The lobster, seeing that it's meal was about to disappear, shot forward. It gripped the dead fish with one of it's massive claws. With three flicks of it's powerful tail the lobster tried to pull the fish away from the eel. Dilo watched. Which one would win the tug-of-war?

It was at this precise moment Dilo felt the explosion.

In an instant the dolphin changed from being idly curious. Dilo became fully alert. He

forgot about the eel, the crab and the lobster. The dolphin sped off in the direction of the sound to investigate.

On the rig there was pandemonium. The drill stopped turning. Sirens were screeching. Men were shouting. Their boots clattered on the catwalks. Blazing oil and gas were spurting into the air. Burning oil was pouring onto the sea and spreading a carpet of orange flame. Clouds of black smoke billowed above the inferno. Being underwater, Dilo was unaware of this.

After the explosion, apart from some extra unusual noises from the rig, under the sea everything was peaceful. But Dilo's curiosity was aroused. He sped towards the rig to find out what was happening.

When he got close Dilo looked up. Above him he saw the glowing yellow flames. He scanned the surface with his sonar. He couldn't understand what was there. He had experienced nothing like it before. He was just about to surface in the midst of the flames to investigate when another sound caught his attention. It was a thrashing sound, like an animal in distress.

Dilo turned and focused his sonar to see what it was. He recognised the shape. It was a human. The human was waving its legs and arms in panic. The human started to sink.

Dilo swam immediately towards the drowning man and pushed him upwards. They surfaced together beside the flaming oil. Dilo sucked in a breath. His lungs were filled with fumes. Dilo's next instinct was to dive and swim away. But something inside the dolphin made him stay.

The choking man started to sink again. Dilo submerged. Using his beak he eased the man, who was losing consciousness, back to the surface and supported him from underneath. Then with the human bundle resting on his back, Dilo swam slowly away from the flames.

As he moved to safety Dilo heard a new

sound. It was getting louder and louder. A strange shape appeared in the sky. The black smoke above the yellow flames swirled into coils. A very strong wind was blowing down from above. Fumes swept over the dolphin and the man he was trying to rescue. Dilo choked when he inhaled. Dilo continued to swim clear of the flaming sea. The wind blew down even stronger. It flattened the water around Dilo and the man. They were in the centre of rings of ripples. Overhead Dilo saw the swirling blades of the helicopter. The din was frightening. But still Dilo stayed supporting the half conscious body from underneath.

A man was being lowered out of the sky on the end of a rope. He plopped gently into the sea beside Dilo and unclipped his harness. He quickly put a strap around the injured man, clipped it to the line, and waved an arm above his head in a circular motion. Within seconds the man who had fallen from the rig was hoisted aloft.

Water from his dripping clothing was scattered by the downdraft. The rescuer watched him being winched up. The moment the limp package reached the hovering helicopter it was hauled inside.

The downdraft from the helicopter fanned the flames. The burning oil was getting closer to the rescuer left in the sea. Dilo swam under the man and came up with his dorsal fin just in front of the man's face, like he did when he gave Debra a tow. The man locked his hands around the fin. Dilo thrust up and down with his tail and pulled the man away from the flames.

The helicopter hovered overhead. The noise was frightening. The water beneath was splashing in all directions. A cable was coming down towards them. Dilo stopped swimming. For a few seconds the dolphin and the man bobbed side by side. The air sea rescuer gently stroked Dilo's head that was glistening red in the light of the fire. The man heard Dilo splutter as the dolphin took a breath.

"Thanks for your help buddy," he gasped as he reached up for the hook and snapped it onto his harness.

As he was being hoisted upwards the man yelled down to Dilo, "This is no place for man nor beast. Get well away from here dolphin."

Dilo started to swim away. But something was wrong. His tail wasn't working properly. His lungs hurt. Normally breathing was quick and easy. Now it was slow and painful.

11 Fire

"Get up Debra, Get up Robin."

It was Uncle Pat.

"Come quickly. There's a fire on the oil rig."

It was dark. The twins put on their dressing gowns and rushed outside. In the bay the night sky was aglow with orange light. Part of the rig was on fire. Flaming oil was spilling down onto the sea. A siren wailed - "Uurp. Uurp. Uurp. Uurp." The sound carried across the still water. It rose up the cliff. The group beside the lighthouse watched in horror.

A patch of sea alongside the rig was on fire.

"Fetch the binoculars," ordered Pat.

Robin ran indoors. He handed the binoculars to his uncle.

"There's been a blow out. Burning oil is pouring over the rig. Here, you have a look," said Pat handing the binoculars to Robin.

"There's someone in the sea," said Robin. "He's floating just beside the flames. The flames are spreading towards him. He's not moving. Yes he is."

The flapping sound of a helicopter in the distance interrupted Robin. Debra took the binoculars from him and looked for the person in the water.

"I can see the man. What's that next to him? It's a fin. It must be Dilo," she cried. "The flames are moving towards them ."

Pat took the binoculars.

"The person in the water is in trouble. He's waving his arms. He's sinking. Dilo's with him. Dilo is trying to push the man away from the flames."

The helicopter roared overhead and sped out to sea towards the rig. Soon it was hovering over the scene. A powerful searchlight beamed down onto the water.

"They are lowering a man from the helicopter," continued Pat handing the binoculars to Debra.

"I can see him quite clearly, he is wearing yellow. He's in the water. He's unclipped himself." Debra paused. "He's putting a loop around the man. Dilo is still there. The flames are spreading towards them The man is being lifted up."

Debra continued to watch as the rescued man was winched up and pulled into the helicopter. As soon as he was on board the loop was lowered again. Debra watched horrified as flames crept towards the crewman who was still in the water. Dilo was by his side. The man put his arm across Dilo's back. Smoke blown by the helicopter swirled around the man and dolphin. For a time they vanished from Debra's view. Then the man re-appeared above a gap in the black cloud. He was strapped in the harness and was being winched up to the helicopter which was already moving away. Below, the swirling dark grey smoke was tinged red by the light from the burning oil.

"The man in yellow is in the helicopter," shouted Debra.

"Where's Dilo?" asked Robin.

"I can't see him. He's somewhere under that smoke," replied Debra, "Can you see him Uncle?" she said handing the binoculars to Pat.

The helicopter moved sideways well away from the smoke and flames. The powerful searchlight that had been beaming down onto the sea was switched off.

"The chopper is well out of danger now. The two people are safely onboard," said Pat as he scanned the sea. "There's no sign of Dilo."

Then, like a giant dragon fly, the helicopter sped away from the blazing rig. Watching from the cliff top the twins and their uncle looked down

on the whirling blades as the chopper raced past the cliffs beneath the lighthouse.

"I expect they're taking whoever fell in the sea to the hospital in the town," said Pat.

A loud thump came from the rig. The flaming oil stopped spurting upwards.

"They've stopped the blow out. The fire fighting crew are getting the burning oil under control," reported Pat

The burning oil slick started to drift away from the rig on the tide.

"I wonder if anyone else on the rig has been injured?" questioned Robin.

"What about Dilo? I do hope he's alright," exclaimed Debra anxiously.

"I hope so too," replied Uncle Pat. "If he was in the middle of that burning oil, he doesn't stand a chance. Even if he was clear of the oil the fumes that would have got into his lungs when he was helping the men in the sea could kill him."

"I can't see a sign of him anywhere," said

Debra anxiously as she scanned the scene with the binoculars.

Robin put his arm over his sister's shoulder. Debra was shaking.

"That dolphin of yours has been in trouble before and he has lived to tell the story," said Robin, trying to console his twin sister.

He was putting on a brave face for the sake of Debra. So too did Pat who wasn't at all sure if Dilo was still alive. Could a dolphin survive the smoke he must have breathed in?

12 A Night Swim

The fire on the rig was out. The flaming oil slick, carried by the tide, was drifting slowly away from the rig towards the open sea.

"It looks as if everything is under control. There's nothing we can do. I think it's time we went back to bed," said Pat.

"I wonder what happened to Dilo?" said Debra as they strolled towards the lighthouse.

Just after she had spoken Debra heard a sound coming from the bottom of the cliff.

"Quiet," she said, holding her finger to her lips. Everyone listened intently. From below came a quiet "Phht".

"I know what that sound is. It's Dilo! He must be near the steps at the bottom of the cliff," cried Debra. "Uncle Pat, can Robin and I go down and see if he's alright? I'll worry all night if we don't."

"Go inside and get the lamp and a torch," instructed her uncle.

Debra disappeared into the house. Once inside she tore off her pyjamas. Within seconds she was dressed and back outside wearing her swimming costume under her dressing gown. Keeping the torch for herself, Debra gave the lamp she was brandishing to Robin who was not sure if he was ready for a nighttime adventure. Their uncle looked uneasy.

"Come on Robin," Debra urged her brother, "or I'll go by myself."

"No you won't," retorted her uncle instantly. "Either you go with Robin, or you don't go at all."

"Oh, alright," said Robin reluctantly.

"Don't be long," said their uncle as the twins set off down the cliff path. "I'll have some cocoa ready for you when you get back. And mind how you go."

"Don't worry, we'll be alright," said Debra. Setting off immediately before her uncle changed his mind.

The air was quite still. The sea gently swished against the rocks. The twins soon reached the bottom of the cliff. Debra shone the torch across the almost silent water.

Suddenly the beam reflected off a silver fin.

"Look," exclaimed Debra. "There he is."

Dilo stayed still on the surface. He took a laboured breath.

"Dilo doesn't usually make that noise when he breathes," said Debra. "There's something wrong with him."

Dilo circled listlessly a short distance from the rocks.

"I'm going to go in to see him," said Debra.

"You can't!" extorted Robin.

"Oh yes I can," said Debra to her astonished brother, as she started to take off her dressing gown. "I've got my costume on. Here, take my torch and put the lamp on the rocks so it shines over the water."

A few moments later Debra slipped into the sea and swam gently forwards. Dilo finned towards her. He coughed out of his blowhole.

"Oh Dilo," said Debra as she came alongside. "We saw you out there when the rig was on fire. Did you breathe in any of those nasty fumes?"

Dilo stayed on the surface. Debra very gently ran her hand over his head.

"Don't worry, I'll look after you," she said reassuringly.

"Come back. Come back," came an anxious cry across the water, "Uncle Pat will be cross if he sees you in the water."

"Goodbye Dilo," said Debra. "I'll come and see you first thing in the morning."

In a few strokes she was back by the steps. Robin was relieved to see his sister climbing back onto the rocks. Debra slipped on her shoes and dressing gown.

"He knows you are good swimmer but I reckon Uncle Pat's going to be mad at you for going in," puffed Robin as they scrambled back up the cliff path.

Pat hadn't noticed that Debra had changed before she scampered down the cliffs. He was shocked when he saw she was in a wet costume. What on earth did the girl think she was up to? He felt it was a stupid thing to do. If he had known what she was about to do he would have certainly stopped her. Nonetheless he secretly admired her for being so brave. And she was back safe and sound. So he decided to forgive her foolishness.

"Go and get changed out of that wet costume at once," he ordered firmly.

Debra did as she was told and returned to the kitchen in her pyjamas and dressing gown. Although he was still angry at her, Pat sensed that his niece was upset and was worrying about Dilo. He handed her a cup of cocoa.

"If Dilo was able to swim to the lighthouse I am sure he will be OK," he said to console Debra. "Anyway there's nothing more we can do now. When you have finished your cocoa you two must go to bed. You've had enough excitement for one night."

Debra remained silent. She didn't want to go to bed. Her thoughts kept going back to the sea. She knew that Dilo wasn't well. Debra wanted to stay up but she was very tired. She walked slowly to her bedroom and crawled into bed. The moment her head touched the pillow Debra fell into a deep sleep.

13 Ghost Dolphins

Dilo watched Debra and Robin climb the cliff path. Then he sank slowly. He liked the way the girl had stroked him. She was very gentle. Now she was gone. It was dark. There was still a lot of noise coming from the rig. But the dolphin wasn't interested. He needed to rest. He swam towards a place where he would be safe.

Mermaid Cove was on the side of the bay opposite the lighthouse. Normally he could get there easily without going up to breathe. Tonight Dilo was very short of breath. He had to surface five times. Each time he sucked in air, his lungs hurt. It seemed to take a long time.

Dilo sent out his magic sound. At last he was getting near. He saw a sound picture of the rocks. There was the gulley he wanted. The dolphin glided between the stone walls that opened into a big pool. It was the place he used to go to when he needed peace. Inside all was quiet. Dilo rested on the surface. He remained still. His breathing got slower and slower. Then it stopped altogether. Dilo slowly sank into the depths. Everything around Dilo went misty. Then through the mist a group of ghost dolphins appeared. They swam gently around him. He wasn't frightened. In fact he felt quite calm. He watched the dolphins gliding silently through the water. Had they come to take him into the next world?

Dilo tried to join them. But he couldn't move. Still the dolphins continued to swim around him with slow regular sweeps of their tails. They were dark grey. There seemed to be nothing between him and them. It was as if they were flying through the air as lazily as seagulls. The circle they were moving in was becoming bigger and bigger. Now they were flying through the rock walls, away from him. Dilo tried to follow them, but his tail wouldn't work. The dolphins were getting further and further away. They were fading. As they disappeared he had a strange feeling inside. Then they vanished as silently as they came. And all was black.

Dilo continued to sink gently into the depths. But a tiny spark of life remained inside him. With a weak move of his tail Dilo stopped sinking and started to drift slowly towards the surface. When Dilo reached the top he took a breath and the spark of life turned into a flame.

Everything was getting clearer. Dilo looked around and could see the steep black rocks that surrounded him. Above them was the deep blue sky. It was speckled with stars. In the stars he saw his mother. Her outline was bright and clear. Dilo could feel her presence, giving him strength. Then Dilo remembered a memory of long ago.

The dolphins he had just seen were the same dolphins who came to him when his mother was caught in a net and died. He remembered how he wanted to go with her into the next world. But they told him it was not his time and that he had a mission. That was why he had a star on his dorsal fin.

Slowly Dilo realised they had come to tell him it was still not time for him to leave this world. His mission was not finished yet.

Seeing his mother in the stars filled Dilo with quiet hope. It was as if she was beside him in the water. He remembered the fun they had had together. He remembered how beautiful she was. He remembered how much she had taught him. How she made stars come out of her tail and showed him he could do it too. That was long ago.

Dilo's breathing was getting easier.

14 Mermaid Cove

Dilo stayed on the surface looking up into the heavens. The sky was slowly getting lighter. The stars were getting dimmer. Dilo watched the image of his mother gradually fade. Even so he could still feel her watching over him. The dark grey sky was turning orange. Brighter and brighter it became. Then the first ray of sunlight touched the top of the cliffs. The grey shadows on the cliffs moved slowly down as the sun climbed higher into a clear blue sky.

A bright new day had arrived. Dilo could feel it feeding life into his body as he cruised around the pool in Mermaid Cove. High above sea birds were sitting on their nests. They were always a bit noisy. Suddenly the noise level rose. They were all squawking. Many of them flew off their nests. The air was filled with screeching birds. Like a cloud of smoke from a chimney they rose into the sky above the cove.

Dilo knew the signal. It spelt danger. Something had frightened the nesting birds. He allowed himself to sink into the dark water of the pool. Then he heard splashes. A boat was coming into the gulley that led to his secret hiding place inside the cliffs.

From under the sea Dilo saw a wooden hull approaching. He recognised the little boat. It was the dinghy from the lighthouse. A voice rose eerily up through the rock chimney.

"Dilo, Dilo," it cried.

"Dilo, Dilo," echoed back.

The voice cried again anxiously.

"Dilo, Dilo."

The dolphin rose slowly. He surfaced beside the boat and took a quick breath. "Phht".

The sudden noise startled Debra.

"Oh," she shrieked when she saw what had

caused it. A look of relief swept across Debra's face. "Oh Dilo, it's you. I was so worried about you. Are you alright?"

She leant over the side of the dinghy and stroked the dome of Dilo's head. Debra was laughing and crying with relief at the same time.

Pat, who had rowed the dinghy across from the lighthouse, sat watching silently as his niece gently caressed Dilo's shiny head. But the effect was not at all what he, or Debra, expected. Without warning the dolphin suddenly swam to the entrance of Mermaid Cove and out through the gulley into Lighthouse Bay.

"Hey, wait for me," shouted Debra.

Pat sprung into action. He put an oar over the stern and skulled out through the narrow passage.

Dilo was waiting for them outside Mermaid Pool. Once they were clear of the rocks Pat rowed strongly across the bay. Debra sat in the stern trailing her hand in the water. Dilo stayed with the boat. Sometimes he swam ahead, At other times he followed behind letting Debra touch his beak.

From the top of the cliffs Robin watched in amazement. He could see Dilo moving around the dinghy as his uncle pulled on the oars. He ran down the steps to greet them.

"Isn't it wonderful," shouted Debra as the boat bumped gently against the rocks. Her eyes filling with tears once again.

"Dilo's safe and sound. He was where I thought he would be - in Mermaid Cove."

Pat tied the painter of his dinghy to a ring on the rocks.

"Thank you, thank you Uncle Pat, for taking me across to Mermaid Cove," she said as they watched Dilo swim away.

"Dilo has certainly made an amazing recovery." said Pat.

"It looks like he's hungry and is going to find some breakfast."

But Pat was wrong.

15 Silver Comes Back

Dilo swam away from the lighthouse steps because he had heard a familiar sound. He swam towards it. Not like he usually did, swiftly underwater. But slowly across the surface of the sea. An inflatable boat was speeding towards him. They met in the middle of the bay.

It was Mike in his inflatable. He cut the engine as soon as he spotted Dilo. The dolphin swam slowly alongside.

"Hello Dilo. Am I pleased to see you. I heard that you had disappeared. The fishermen said that you probably died in the fire. Are you going to come with me to the lighthouse?"

"Mike, Mike," came a voice across the water.

It was Debra. She was jumping up and down

frantically waving her arms in the air.

Mike waved back to Debra and started his engine. The inflatable moved gently forward with Dilo swimming alongside. When they reached the steps Mike jumped ashore and tied up his boat next to Pat's wooden dinghy. As soon as the rope was secure Debra threw herself at Mike and gave him a big hug.

"Oh Michael, I'm so pleased to see you," she said. "And Dilo has come with you."

Debra then launched into the story of how she and her uncle had found Dilo in Mermaid Cove.

"Dilo wasn't the only victim of the fire on the rig," said Mike stepping back into his boat. He bent down and picked up a lobster pot. Crouched in the bottom were two bedraggled seabirds - a guillemot and a seagull. They raised their heads as Mike put the pot on the rocks. Debra could see that their eyes were bright but their feathers were covered with oil.

"A fisherman spotted these two on his way out to the fishing grounds," said Mike. "He knew about International Wildlife Watch. So he called me up and asked if I would bring them over to Pat. Do you think you can save them?" he asked, holding up the pot for Pat to take a closer look.

"Let's take them up to the Rescue Room," replied Pat. "The seagull is not too badly oiled but the guillemot looks in poor shape."

Debra took a last look at Dilo.

"I'll be back to see you later," she said before she started to climb up the cliff path.

In his small laboratory Pat untied the door of the lobster pot, carefully lifted out the guillemot and put the bird in the sink. Debra, Robin and Mike watched as the guillemot flapped around weakly, leaving smears of oil in the sink. It opened and shut it's beak. Then it slowly sank and lay quite still. Pat picked it up, gently supporting it's lifeless head. He sighed and looked sad.

"I'm afraid it's gone", he said as he placed

the dead guillemot on the draining board.

The others looked on anxiously as Pat then reached for the seagull. It was much more lively than the guillemot and it pecked at Pat as he placed it in the sink. It fell clumsily with a disgruntled squawk as it tried to stand. Robin, who was watching closely shouted with amazement. "It's only got one leg. It's Silver!"

"Well I'll be blowed," said Pat with a gasp. "You're right Robin!"

The seagull continued to peck sharply at his arm as Pat started to wipe the oil off Silver's feathers.

"Ouch!" said Pat after a particularly vicious bite. "There's gratitude for you. If Silver is strong enough to bite me like that I reckon he's going to be alright!"

"Do you think Silver knew he would be rescued and that you would look after him?" asked Robin.

"Oh yes," replied Pat with his eyes

sparkling.

"How?"

"By telepathy of course!"

The next day Robin dug a grave for the guillemot on the top of the cliffs. Silver hopped around on one leg picking up worms. When Robin had finished Debra put a stone on the grave and said a little prayer. As she murmured the words Silver opened his wings and glided out over the sea.

Debra loved watching gulls flying. They seemed so free. Seeing Silver reminded her of Percy the penguin.

"I'm going to say a prayer for Percy locked up in the zoo," said Debra.

"Penguins can't fly like seagulls," said Robin.

"I know that," replied Debra. "But all birds should be free."

"Hm," said Robin, thoughtfully, "I think we should keep quiet about Percy."

16 Equipment Check

When the twins arrived back at the lighthouse after burying the guillemot Mike was in the kitchen having a cup of tea with Pat.

"I knew you'd be here," said Debra. "I saw your inflatable tied up at the bottom of the steps."

"I've been telling your uncle about a new diving job I've been offered," said Mike taking a sip of tea. "A fishing boat, overladen with fish, has been swamped by a freak wave. The crew were all able to get off in the lifeboat before it sank. The owners want me to find it, survey it, and see if it can be salvaged."

"Where did this happen?" asked Robin

"Somewhere off Deadman Point."

"That's not too far away," said Pat.

"I'm heading there now in Merlin. Before I

go I want to make sure that all of my equipment is working properly. So I wondered if you would all like to come on board and check it out with me?"

"Oh yes please," blurted Robin before his uncle could reply.

"We're anchored in fairly shallow water. I thought Debra might like to go for a dive?"

Debra's eyes lit up.

"Oh yes! yes! yes!" she said clasping her hands together in excitement. "I'd love to. When can we go?"

"As soon as you are ready if your Uncle Pat agrees."

In a flurry of excitement Debra rushed off to get her wetsuit, fins, mask and snorkel.

Soon they were all on board the inflatable heading out to Merlin expecting Dilo to come alongside. But he didn't.

"I hope Dilo is alright," said Mike.

"He was fine this morning. I had a swim with him," said Debra cheerfully.

"It's strange that he hasn't come to the inflatable," commented Mike as he drew up alongside Merlin.

"Then I'll send Dilo a message by telepathy and ask him to come and dive with us," said Debra seriously.

Robin looked at Mike and sighed. He didn't have to say anything. Mike knew what Robin was thinking.

Charlie, Mike's crewman, was waiting for them. A soon as they were all on board Charlie helped Debra put on an aqualung.

"Do you remember the signals Mike taught you?" he asked.

Debra knew that divers could not talk to each other underwater. Mike and Pat watched as she rehearsed her hand signals with Charlie. Her twin brother had disappeared inside the boat.

Robin heard two splashes as Debra and Charlie jumped overboard. A few moments later Pat and Mike joined Robin in the wheelhouse.

"Right," said Mike. "First we'll check the GPS - that's Global Positioning System. It tells us exactly where we are."

A screen displayed a map of the coast. Mike twiddled a knob. The picture jumped.

"That's Lighthouse Bay," said Mike. "Look, there's the town and the jetty. And here's the lighthouse."

Robin watched him, fascinated. Mike turned the knob again. The picture jumped. The only area shown was Black Rock and the cliffs beneath the lighthouse.

"We are exactly here," said Mike triumphantly, pointing to a red arrow in the middle of the screen. "Now let's go underwater," he continued, turning to another display with jagged bands of different colours running across the screen. "Look, there's the seabed. And that's how deep it is. Eight metres."

Mike flicked a switch and two blotches of colour moved in jerks across the screen.

"That's Debra and Charlie," he said, "but oh, ho, what's this?"

Mike looked intently at the screen.

"There's something else down there with them," he said. "And it's big."

"I hope it's not a shark," said Robin who was scared of sharks.

"There aren't any sharks round here," said Mike, "It can only be Dilo."

When Debra jumped into the sea she was surrounded by a cloud of bubbles. She waited for them to clear. When they did she saw Charlie beside her. Debra held up her hand and made a circle with her thumb and forefinger. It was the signal that she was OK. Charlie made the same sign back. It was time for them to set off on their dive together.

Debra took hold of the anchor rope and pulled herself along it. Each time she breathed out Debra heard her bubbles gurgling out of her regulator. Then, in one of the silent periods between breaths, she heard another sound. "Eek, eek."

Debra turned her head sharply left and right. Suddenly she felt as if her body was full of bubbles - like fizzy lemonade. It was Dilo's sonar. In the misty distance she could see Dilo heading in her direction. Slowly at first. Then the dolphin pumped his tail quickly up and down and sped towards her.

Dilo whizzed past Debra, turned around, and flew back towards her again. He didn't stop. He swam underneath her and followed the rope, and then the anchor chain that was stretched across the sandy seabed. Debra chased after him. When she caught up Dilo was hanging tail up over the anchor wagging his head from side to side.

In her mind Debra could hear her dolphin friend saying, "Come on slowcoach. Look what I've found. An anchor!"

Dilo then set off to tell those on the boat of his discovery. He flicked his tail as hard as he

could and rushed upwards. Debra watched him rocket towards the surface. For a moment the dolphin disappeared as he leapt into the air. Then Dilo burst back into the sea and sped to the anchor.

In the wheelhouse Robin, Mike and Pat were watching Dilo over the anchor on the echo sounder screen. Then to their amazement, at the same moment, through the wheelhouse window, they saw the dolphin flying through the air.

"There's a slight time delay on the echo sounder," explained Mike after they heard Dilo splash back into the sea. "He's gone now. And look, here he is again!" continued Mike when Dilo reappeared on the screen. "He's going back to the anchor.".

"You were right Mike," said Robin when he had got over the shock of suddenly seeing Dilo flying through the air beside the boat. "It must have been Dilo we saw on the echo sounder."

"By the way that dolphin is behaving it

looks like he's made a full recovery," added Pat.

Debra came to the same conclusion as she and Dilo swam away from the anchor and into a rocky gulley. Debra gazed at all the creatures on the rocks. Breathing from her aqualung she could hover and look at them carefully. Debra stretched her finger towards what looked like a tiny umbrella made of feathers sticking out of the rocks. Dilo was watching over her shoulder. Suddenly all of the feathers disappeared. All that was left was a grey tube.

"Ah, she's discovered a plop, plop," said Dilo to himself.

Dilo swam beside Debra as she peered into the nooks and crannies. She had forgotten all about Charlie, who was keeping a careful eye on her. She jumped when he tapped her on the shoulder. He signalled her to follow him.

Charlie hovered in front of a small cave and pointed towards it. Debra sank down and peered in. Charlie switched on his underwater torch. The beam shone onto a beautiful blue lobster, mottled with creamy white patches. Two long feelers stretched towards the divers sensing their presence. It's eyes glowed reflecting the torch light. Two large claws were ready for action. The lobster moved menacingly forward. It stopped at the entrance to the cave. Dilo got excited and wagged his head up and down. Debra continued to watch the lobster from a safe distance. Then Charlie pointed upwards. It was time to return to the boat.

After tea in the saloon Mike ferried Pat and the twins back to the lighthouse steps. They waved to him from the top of the cliffs as Merlin headed out of the bay towards Deadman Point.

17 Special News

The next day was the last day of the twin's holiday. Debra spent as much time as she could with Dilo. Sometimes they would rush around together as fast as they could go. At other times their games were very gentle. When they floated quietly on the surface Debra talked to Dilo, just as if he was a human friend. On their final swim together in the afternoon Debra told Dilo she had some special news.

"We had a visitor at lunchtime. He said you saved his life. He was the man you rescued from the oil rig. His name is Frank. He is ever so nice. He told us he had heard some confidential information. Which means he shouldn't really tell us. He said that the rig had come to explore for oil. We all knew that of course. Then he told us that despite the blow out they hadn't found much oil."

Dilo swam slowly around Debra as if he was paying attention.

"He said that he had heard that the oil under Lighthouse Bay was not economically viable. I'm not quite sure what that means. But I think it means it won't make much money. So they're going to move out. That's great news isn't it?"

Dilo blew out. "Phht."

"I'll take that as a 'Yes'," said Debra.

Debra didn't like saying "Goodbye". So she didn't tell Dilo she was leaving. But deep inside Dilo knew.

Ever since the fire on the rig Dilo had been feeling the urge to move on. Now he was better he could follow the 'Call of the Deep' once again. It was time for him to leave too.

Early next morning Dilo headed out of Lighthouse Bay. On the cliff top, beside the lighthouse, a girl, carrying a suitcase, waved and called out, "Goodbye Dilo."

18 Deadman Point

Dilo hadn't got very far out of Lighthouse Bay when he heard some noises that sounded interesting. Being curious, he swam to investigate. He turned on his magic sound. It showed two objects. As Dilo got closer he recognised the first sonar image. It was the hull of Merlin. He surfaced alongside. There was nobody on board. The dolphin followed the rope hanging from the bow and swam to the anchor. Dilo liked anchors. He inspected it carefully before heading towards the sounds that had first attracted his attention a short distance away.

There to his surprise he saw another boat about the same size as Merlin. But instead of being on the surface it was resting on the sea bed. The noises came from Mike and Charlie who were tying a big floppy bag to the anchor winch. They were so busy working that they didn't notice Dilo arrive.

The dolphin wanted to see exactly what they were doing of course. So he continued forward and poked his beak between the two divers. It made them both jump. In the split second before they recognised Dilo, Mike and Charlie thought they were being attacked by a shark.

"Oh, it's you Dilo," said Mike with relief through his mouthpiece, when he realised that the shark was a friendly dolphin. "Please don't barge in like that again Dilo. You frightened the life out of me!"

When he had recovered from his shock, Mike stroked Dilo. The dolphin wagged his head up and down excitedly. To Dilo it seemed that Mike and Charlie were inviting him to join in a new game.

Unfortunately for Dilo that wasn't the case. The two divers had a job to get on with. They couldn't take time off to play. Dilo felt quite put out when they ignored him and continued working.

After watching for a few minutes the dolphin decided to invent his own game. Because they were working hard Mike and Charlie were producing lots of exhaust air from their regulators. So Dilo hovered above them letting their bubbles flow over his body. They tickled. Dilo couldn't laugh like a human of course. But he could wriggle, like a child being tickled. When Mike looked up and saw what Dilo was doing he laughed. That produced even more bubbles.

Having enjoyed his "bubble tickle" Dilo decided it was time to look around the sunken boat. He poked his head into the wheelhouse. He inspected the big drum that hauled in the nets. Next he sank down under the hull and looked at the rudder and propeller that were partly buried in the sand. Then he swam back to Mike and Charlie who were now tying another lifting bag to a cleat on the sunken fishing boat.

19 Email

Debra found out what Dilo had been doing six days after she got back home. Robin opened his email, which he always did as soon as he got up. It was a message from Mike.

Dear Robin and Debra,

I'm sitting at the computer on Merlin at Deadman Point.

The last few days have been pretty exciting. After we left you, Charlie and I soon found the sunken fishing boat. It was resting on an even keel on a flat sandy seabed. It looked just like a parked car. We inspected it but could see no damage and decided to try to raise it to the surface using lifting bags. These are giant bags that you take down empty. After they are fixed into position you fill them with air. If you use enough of them they float upwards pulling up whatever they are attached to. Our first task was to tie lifting bags to parts of the boat that could take the strain.

We had just got started when guess who turned up? Dilo. He suddenly poked his head between Charlie and me. Even though we know there are no sharks in the area he gave us a terrible fright. He obviously wanted to play but we couldn't stop working. So he decided to play in our exhaust bubbles. I guess for him it was like being in a Jacuzzi!

We couldn't tie lifting bags to any parts of the wreck that couldn't take the strain. That would be disastrous. So what we decided to do was to tunnel under the boat using high a power water jet. And then pass heavy straps, called strops, under the boat.

Dilo absolutely loved watching all that was going on. Sometimes we turned the water jet towards him. He would rush away, then come back for more. I've taken some film with my underwater video camera. I'll put it on a DVD and send it to you so you can see what has been happening.

All the bags are now in place with just a little air in them. The weather is set fair for a few days. We will start the final lift tomorrow. That's going to be the moment of truth. If I've done my calculations right the sunken fishing boat should be back on the surface tomorrow afternoon.

I can hear Dilo splashing around outside. When I've sent this email to you I'll go out and see him. After that I'm going for a good night's sleep. Tomorrow is going to be another exciting day. Good Night.

Mike.

"You couldn't send a message like that by telepathy," said Robin, pleased to score a point over his sister.

"I have to admit computers do have their uses at times," Debra replied.

"What's more I can send a reply instantly," continued Robin. "If I had sent it last night, by the time Mike had got back from saying "Goodnight" to Dilo, he could have read it on his computer"

"Well let's send a reply now. Tell Mike how much we enjoyed getting his news, and that we look forward to his next report. I will send a message to Dilo by telepathy."

"I'll stick to email," said Robin

20 Ginger's Sculpture

Dilo spent the same night Mike sent the email to the twins cruising around Merlin. He didn't bother to feed. He liked adventures. Dilo felt something exciting was going to happen. He wasn't disappointed.

Early next morning Dilo heard the air generator start up on Merlin. A few minutes later Charlie was in the water pulling a long pressure hose with him. He swam from bag to bag putting air in each. By mid morning the fishing boat was surrounded by bright yellow bags that looked like helium filled balloons. They didn't sway. They were all pulling straight upwards with enormous force.

After a coffee break it was Mike's turn to go in.

"I reckon she's about ready to come up," said Charlie.

As soon as Mike was in the sea, Dilo swam towards him. The dolphin and the diver swam around the wreck together. Mike checked to see that the bags were all evenly filled. He surfaced and Charlie handed him the air pressure hose. Mike pointed the hose towards Dilo and squirted a burst of air. Dilo did an underwater somersault with delight. Then Mike got down to the serious business of putting small amounts of air into each bag, knowing at this stage he had to be very careful.

As he watched Mike squirt air out of the hose up into a lifting bag, Dilo had an idea.

"I can do that," he said to himself.

To prove it Dilo blew a stream of bubbles out of the blowhole on the top of his head. As he watched the air bubbles rise he decided it worked rather well. His experiment inspired Dilo. The dolphin sped to the surface, snatched a breath of

air and returned to Mike who was cautiously filling the last of the lifting bags.

Dilo swam slowly past Mike until his head was under the giant bag. then the dolphin blew out through his blowhole.

The effect was like tipping scales.

Dilo's bubbles produced the final lift needed to raise the boat. The straps on the big yellow lifting bag quivered. The whole bag shook. Dilo backed quickly away. As he did so the boat started to rise. Slowly at first. Then faster and faster.

Mike watched the wreck rise like a ghost ship in front of him. First he saw the hull sliding upwards. A moment later he was looking at the underside of the boat. Then the keel stretched before him. Sand and silt were falling from it in clouds. At the end of the keel Mike briefly saw the propeller and rudder before they disappeared in brown mist.

Then, quite suddenly, the boat stopped moving. Everything was still. Mike gazed in awe.

The once proud fishing boat was back on the surface.

Dilo was absolutely delighted with this unexpected turn of events. He shot back and forth through the clouds of murky water left behind by the rising boat.

On the deck of Merlin Charlie was equally surprised. First some small buoys burst through the surface. Then the cabin roof of the fishing boat suddenly reared out of the sea. It was followed by the hull which was festooned with lifting bags. Water poured out through the scuppers. A few moments later Mike's head appeared beside the fishing boat that had risen from the depths.

"We've done it! We've done it Mike!" yelled Charlie.

Mike waved back with the air hose.

Dilo joined in the jubilation as only he knew how. He did a series of three leaps one after the other. Mike climbed back on board Merlin. He and Charlie danced round the deck whooping with delight. They'd done it!

Dilo did another three jumps to celebrate.

Debra and Robin got the news by email the same night. Mike told them how the boat had come to the surface. In his email he wrote what happened next.

We secured all the bags that acted as buoys keeping the boat afloat. Then we clambered on board. The stench of rotting fish was terrible. We immediately started pumping out the hull. As we got rid of the water inside the boat rose higher and higher. When she was safely afloat we removed the buoyancy bags. She is still fairly low in the water because of the cargo of rotting fish. The stench is unbelievable. So we've anchored Merlin a little way off. Even so I stink! Charlie stinks! Everything stinks of rotting fish! But we are happy. Tomorrow we'll start shovelling out the fish that remain in the hull which means we'll stink even more. We feel like pirates who have just captured a very smelly prize. We've spliced the mainbrace and are ready to collapse into our bunks. Dilo is still swimming around outside. Goodnight

Mike

Robin and Debra got more news two weeks later in an email from Pat. It told them how Mike had triumphantly towed the fishing boat back into the harbour and had cleaned it up. The email continued:

The smell of fish has gone completely. The boat is being refitted and guess what? Mike is setting up a new business. There's no sign of Dilo. He swam away after the boat was raised. But the fishermen say there are lots of other dolphins about. So Mike is going to convert the fishing boat for diving and dolphin watching trips.

But that's not all Mike's been doing. He's been working with the oil company ferrying materials out to Peak Rock. They've built a concrete plinth on top of it. Yesterday a helicopter lowered a big sculpture of a dolphin onto it. We can see it clearly from the lighthouse. It's an abstract, which means it isn't shaped exactly like a real dolphin. But it certainly touches the heart. I've attached a couple of pictures as jpegs for you to look at.

A plaque has been fixed to the rocks at the half water mark. This means that sailors going past at low water can see it. And divers exploring the gulleys around Peak Rock will be able to read it when the tide is in.

The sculpture was made by Ginger Gilmour ASWA. I've found out that

ASWA stands for Association of Women Artists. I wonder what you think of that?

The Spirit of Dilo

Sculpture by Ginger Gilmour ASWA

To commemorate the rescue of Frank

Gibson by a friendly dolphin

known as Dilo
www.gingerart.net

"I think it's absolutely fabulous," exclaimed Debra when she and Robin saw the jpeg photograph on his computer screen.

"She might have made it look a bit more like a proper dolphin," said Robin

"Oh, you've got no soul," said Debra.

"You've heard someone else say that," retorted Robin.

"That's true," replied Debra, "but I'm sure when people see the sculpture they will feel Dilo's spirit. I do, just by looking at the photo."

"Women," said Robin with a shrug of his shoulders. "I'll never understand them."

"You've heard a grown-up say that haven't you?"

Robin didn't answer. But he knew it was true.

THE END

Extract from Dilo's Fun & Activities Book
Watch publishing ISBN 09522389 1 8
www.idw.org

Rico has made 14 changes to this drawing.....

......Can you spot them?
Colour in the picture when you've added the changes

Caption Dilo's T-Shirt

Design a Dilo T-Shirt

Extract from
Dilo's Fun and Activities Book
Watch Publishing ISBN: 09522389 1 8
www.idw.org

Dear Reader

Have you ever thought how much work goes into a book, apart from just writing it? It's lots I can tell you.

I enjoy writing, especially on long distance flights. When I get back home I call in to see Kirsty at Redcliff Print & Design and present her with pages of untidy scribble and crossings out. This she converts into very neat script. I then contact a good friend, who has shared many dolphin adventures with me. He's an artist as well as diver. His name is Rico. Between us we work out the illustrations.

I'm not very good at spelling and punctuation. So various other friends are called upon to have a look at the draft manuscript. Eventually, when all the corrections are done, Richard at Redcliff puts the book to bed, as they say.

It would be nice to think that the job finishes there. But it doesn't. Now comes what can be the most difficult part of all. Selling it. Before that can happen the printed books must be stored, advertised and distributed. Then, most importantly, someone has to be persuaded to part with their cash to buy it. Not until then will a book get into a reader's hands, which was the aim of writing it in the first place.

I send my deepest thanks to all those who have helped me to put Dilo in Lighthouse Bay into your hands.

Sharing is one of the greatest pleasures in life. I therefore have a request. Please pass on this book to someone else to enjoy. Thank you.

Wishes for Happy Dolphin Days